MATZAH BALL

A PASSOVER STORY

Mindy Avra Portnoy
illustrated by
Katherine Janus Kahn

Kar-Ben Copies, Inc.   Rockville, MD

*To the memory of
two great baseball fans,
Nate Portnoy and Frank J. Breen, Jr.
—MAP*

*To my son Robert
and my brother Edward
who love baseball.
—KJK*

Library of Congress Cataloging-in-Publication Data

Portnoy, Mindy Avra.
    Matzah ball/Mindy Avra Portnoy: illustrated by Katherine Janus Kahn.
       p.   cm.
    Summary: Aaron can't pass up a chance to attend an Orioles game at Camden Yards.
even though it's during Passover and he'll have to bring special food.
    ISBN 0-929371-68-2 (hc) — ISBN 0-929371-69-0 (pbk): [1. Passover—Fiction.
2. Baseball—Fiction. 3. Judaism—Customs and practices—Fiction. 4. Jews—United
States—Fiction.] I. Kahn, Katherine, ill. II. Title.
PZ7.P8375Mat   1994
[E]—dc20
                                    93-39402
                                    CIP
                                    AC

Published by KAR-BEN COPIES, INC. Rockville. MD 1-800-4-KARBEN
Printed in the United States of America.

Traditionally, Elijah the Prophet is associated with the holiday of Passover. At the festive seder meal, the Cup of Elijah, filled with wine, is placed in the center of the table, and the door is opened in the hope that the prophet will enter to herald the messianic era. Elijah is also the hero of many folktales. It is said that he never died, but wanders the earth to bring comfort, solace, and even miracles.

It's not always easy being Jewish, but sometimes it can lead to miracles. It happened to me last year at an Orioles game at Camden Yards.

Larry's dad had tickets to an early season game, and Larry had invited Dan, Kate, and me to go along. We're on a neighborhood softball team together, and he knew we'd really enjoy watching the O's clobber the Rangers.

I was telling my mom how excited I was, when her voice shattered my visions of home runs flying way out to Eutaw Street.

"Don't forget, Aaron, the game is during Passover. No hot pretzels, no crackerjacks, no ice cream. You'll have to bring your own food."

"Aw, mom," I groaned. "How can you enjoy a baseball game without junk food? The other kids aren't Jewish, and they'll be able to eat anything they like. It's not fair."

"Sorry, Aaron," she answered. "Those are the rules."

I was really mad. It's not easy being Jewish, and sometimes it feels downright weird. Every year, I have to explain why there's a sukkah in my backyard, and why I'm always missing great TV shows on Shabbat. My friends think I'm lucky because I get extra days off from school, and they say I have it made because Hanukkah lasts for eight days, but I'm not so sure. Sometimes, I wish I could be just like everyone else.

Mom wasn't finished lecturing, of course. She told me how lucky I was to be able to celebrate Passover, and reminded me that there were many times and places when Jews had to eat matzah in secret. She also pointed out that the Jewish slaves in Egypt had suffered a lot more than I would suffer by not eating crackerjacks for one whole ballgame. But I was still unconvinced. After all, they didn't even have baseball when the rabbis wrote down all the rules about Passover food. I'm sure they'd have made an exception.

The day of the game was perfect — sunny and cool. Mom packed me a Passover lunch: matzah, tuna fish in a container, chocolate chip macaroons, and those disgusting, sugary fruit slices.

When I arrived at Larry's house, he wanted to know what was in my bag.

"It's my lunch," I grumbled. "It's Passover, so I can't eat the usual stuff at the ballpark."

"Oh, too bad," he said, then suddenly his face brightened. "Do you have any of those great-tasting Passover cookies?"

"You mean macaroons? Of course," I answered. "What else do you think my mom would have packed?"

"I love macaroons," Larry drooled.

"Okay, okay, Larry, I'll let you have some at the ballpark," I assured him as I followed him out to the car.

We drove to Camden Yards. Larry's father even had a special parking permit so we could get into one of the lots near the stadium. We joined the flood of people going in. Lines were already forming at the food concessions and wonderful smells filled the air. We bought our scorecards, found our seats, and settled in for the game.

Three pitches into the first inning, Larry reminded me about the macaroons. "Oooh, you have macaroons!" sighed Kate. "I love macaroons." She began to rummage through my lunch bag and found the fruit slices. "These look good, too. Let's share." My lunch was fast disappearing, but I wasn't so hot on macaroons and fruit slices anyway.

The game was a baseball triumph and a culinary disaster. The Orioles scored run after run. Ripken was tremendous, Anderson was fabulous, Devereaux was dazzling. . .and I was starving.

It turned out Larry's dad has a thing for matzah, so I gave him some of mine.

Thanks to Dan, the tuna fish was gone by the second inning. My friends were happily devouring my lunch, as well as every bit of chametz* in the ballpark.

By the fifth inning, I was so hungry I began to fantasize about opening a special "Kosher for Passover" food stand at Oriole Park. I prayed that the game wouldn't go into extra innings.

* Bread products and other foods not eaten on Passover.

In the top of the eighth, the Rangers had a pitching change. My friends decided to head out to the concession stands one last time. I stayed behind, feeling sorry for myself.

Suddenly, I felt someone tapping on my shoulder, and turned to see that an old man had sat down next to me.

"Hi," he said. "I noticed your lunch bag. It reminds me of
when my mother used to pack a Passover lunch for me
when we'd go out to Ebbets Field."

"You were at Ebbets Field?" my mouth dropped open.

"Sure," he said. "Those were the good old days. Tons of
matzah and macaroons all over the place. You weren't
distracted with buying junk food and could concentrate on
the game. Know what I mean?"

"Yeah, I guess so," I answered.

And suddenly I saw myself part of that Ebbets Field gang. All those Jewish kids eating their Passover lunches, watching Jackie Robinson stealing second. I didn't feel so alone anymore.

"I still bring my own lunch," he said. "Here, would you like another piece of matzah?"

"Thanks," I said, and turned back to the game. I ignored the singsong of the peanut vendor and kept my eyes on the field.

The new Rangers pitcher wasn't helping his team out at all. The O's had guys at the corners, on a walk and a single up the middle, bobbled by the second baseman.

Cal was up to bat. A fast ball whizzed by for strike one.

He fouled the next one off the first base line. Two balls followed. The old guy next to me whispered a prayer, "Just one home run, Cal. *Dayenu*.* That will be enough."

* The Hebrew word for "enough." The title of a traditional seder song.

Then, I heard the crack of the bat, and saw the ball heading in our direction. It was too late to grab my glove. The matzah was all I had. It would have to be enough.

I held it up in the air, and heard the old man yell, "It's yours, Aaron!" The ball shattered the matzah into a million pieces. . . and fell into my lap. I clutched it and turned to thank him, but he had disappeared.

Where had he gone? He'd just been there. I had the matzah — or at least the crumbs — to prove it.

When my friends returned, they nearly fainted when they saw the ball. "Congratulations!" Larry's dad said. "Aren't you lucky you weren't standing out in the concession line with us."

Now if someone tells me there's no such thing as a miracle, I just smile and show them my matzah ball. I wonder, though, sometimes when I look at it, whatever happened to my friend from Ebbets Field? And, come to think of it, how did he know my name?